PUFFIN BOOKS

Published by the Penguin Group
Penguin Books Ltd, 80 Strand, London WC2R 0RL, England
Penguin Putnam Inc., 375 Hudson Street, New York, New York 10014, USA
Penguin Books Australia Ltd, 250 Camberwell Road, Camberwell, Victoria 3124, Australia
Penguin Books Canada Ltd, 10 Alcorn Avenue, Toronto, Ontario, Canada M4V 3B2
Penguin Books India (P) Ltd, 11 Community Centre, Panchsheel Park, New Delhi – 110 017, India
Penguin Books (NZ) Ltd, Cnr Rosedale and Airborne Roads, Albany, Auckland, New Zealand
Penguin Books (South Africa) (Pty) Ltd, 24 Sturdee Avenue, Rosebank 2196, South Africa

Penguin Books Ltd, Registered Offices: 80 Strand, London WC2R 0RL, England

www.penguin.com

First published by Hamish Hamilton 1985
Published in Puffin Books 1995
15 17 19 20 18 16

Made and printed in Italy by Printer Trento Srl

British Library Cataloguing in Publication Data
A CIP catalogue record for this book is available from the British Library

0–140–55556–0

Knock Knock Who's There?

by Sally Grindley
Illustrated by Anthony Browne

PUFFIN BOOKS

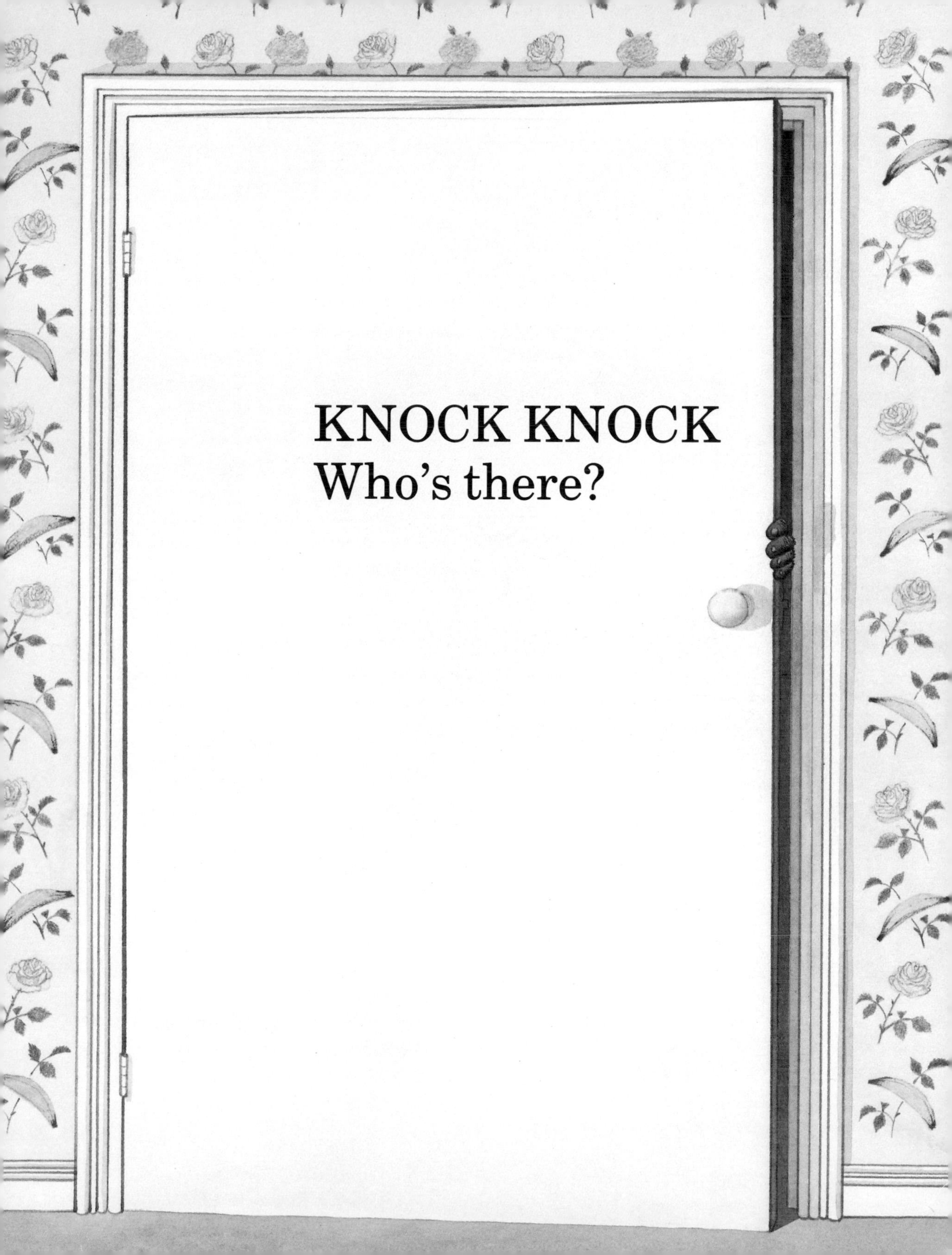

KNOCK KNOCK
Who's there?

I'm a great big GORILLA
with fat furry arms
and huge white teeth.

When you let me in,
I'm going to hug your breath away!

Then I WON'T let you in!

KNOCK KNOCK
Who's there?

I'm a wicked old WITCH
with a long pointed hat
and a wand full of magic.

When you let me in,
I'm going to turn you into a frog!

Then I WON'T let you in!

KNOCK KNOCK
Who's there?

I'm a very creepy GHOST
with a face as white as a sheet
and chains that jangle and clank.

When you let me in,
I'm going to SPOOK you!

Then I WON'T let you in!

KNOCK KNOCK
Who's there?

I'm a fierce scaly DRAGON
with smoke up my nose
and fire in my mouth.

When you let me in,
I'm going to cook you for my tea!

Then I WON'T let you in!

KNOCK KNOCK
Who's there?

I'm the world's tallest GIANT
with eyes like footballs
and feet like a football pitch.

When you let me in,
I'm going to tread on you!

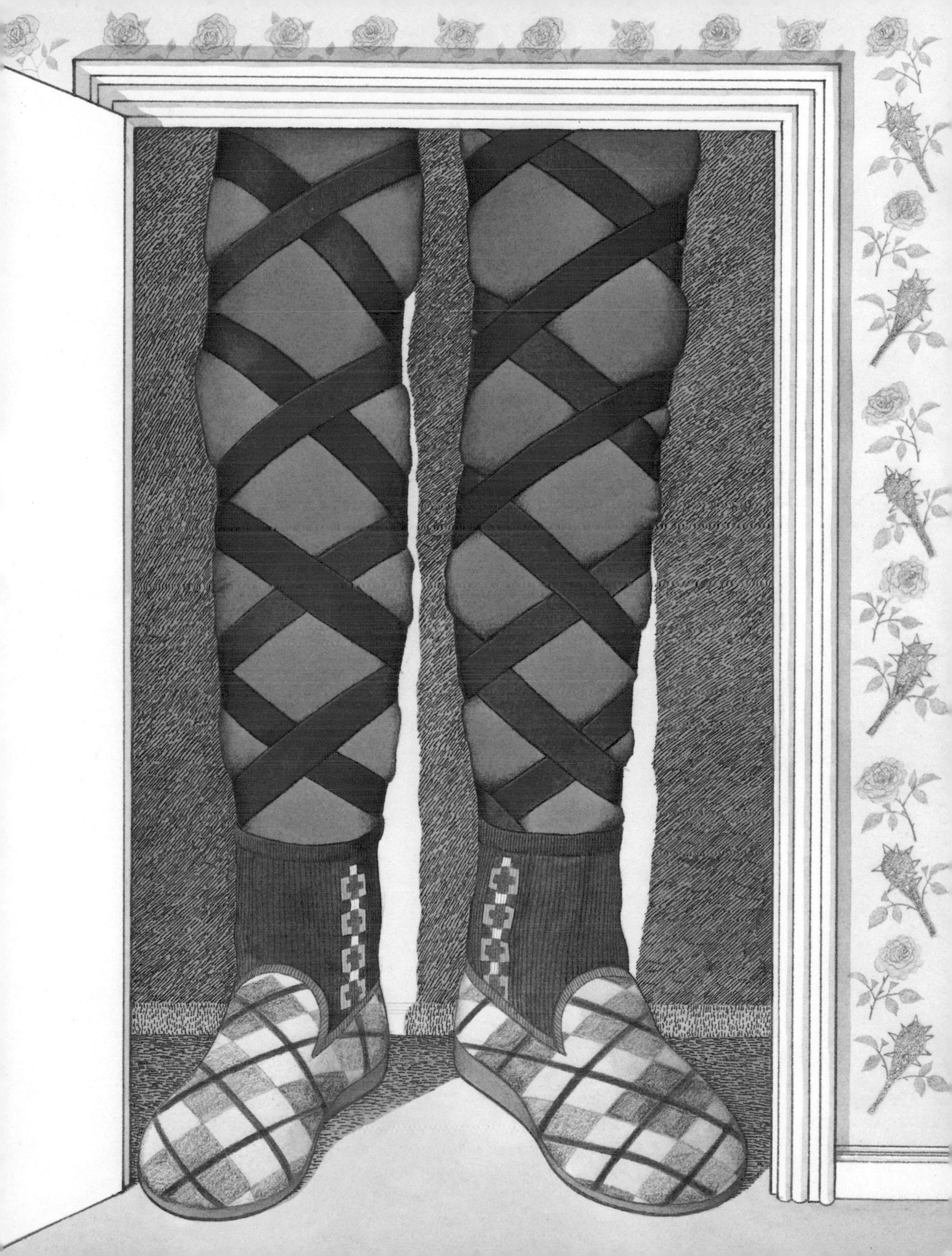

Then I WON'T let you in!

KNOCK KNOCK
Who's there?

I'm your big cuddly daddy
with a mug of hot chocolate
and a story to tell.

PLEASE may I come in?

COME IN, COME IN, COME IN,

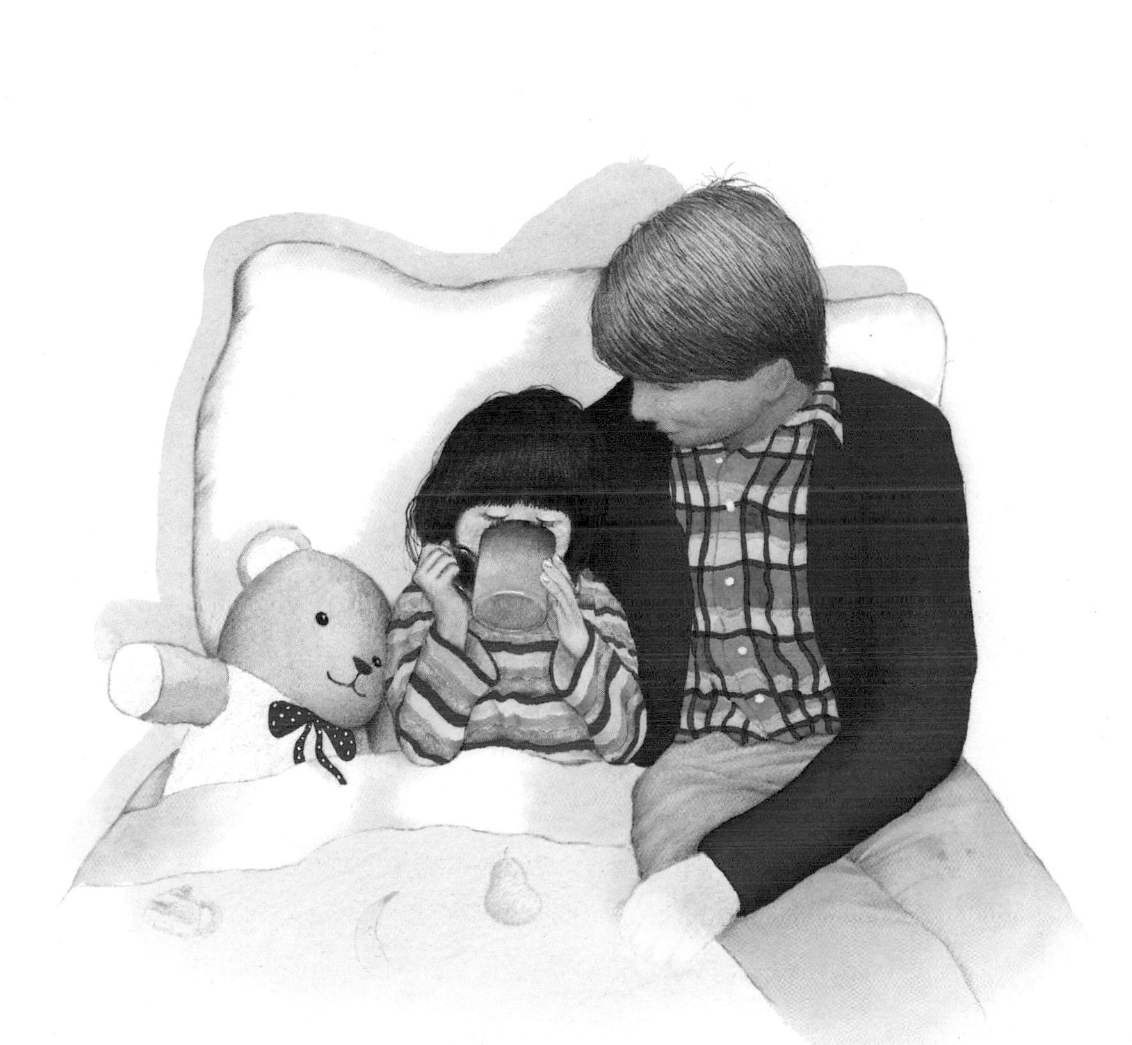

There's been a gorilla at the door,
and a witch
and a ghost
and a dragon
and a giant
and . . .

I knew it was you . . . really.